KING FOR EVER!

KING FOR EVER!

CYPRIAN EKWENSI

Copyright © 1992, 2023 by Cyprian Ekwensi

All rights reserved by Maria Chinwe Ekwensi, Laura Njideka Ekwensi, David Onochie Ekwensi, within the named rights in the estate of the late Cyprian Ekwensi by his last will. No part of this book may be reproduced or transmitted in any form or by any means, electronic or mechanical, including photocopying, recording, or any information storage and retrieval system, without permission. For more information, please reach out to info@cyprianekwensibooks.com.

ISBN: 978-1-960611-04-8 - Paperback
eISBN: 978-1-960611-05-5 - eBook

Library of Congress Control Number: 2023908042

Cover Illustration by Nancy Batra

∞This paper meets the requirements of ANSI/NISO Z39.48-1992 (Permanence of Paper)

050323

1

The kingdom of Bamanga was once ruled by a monarch called Sinanda. Sinanda had not been born into a royal family. He did not look or walk like a king. He did not have the dignity of a king. But he was a very tall man, and he had a very tough appearance.

Sinanda had joined the Royal Army of Bamanga when he was fifteen. His family was poor, like most families in Bamanga. There were few jobs and little chance for a good education. He had told his mother that he would work hard. He said that one day he would become an officer and that she would be proud of him.

People laughed when his mother told them, but his mother knew that Sinanda had been clever. First of all, she knew the army would give Sinanda good food, free clothes, a free education and free accommodation in the barracks. He would receive a weekly wage. This would support him and help the family.

Second, the army was very important in Bamanga. If Sinanda did well, he could make a good career for himself and provide money for the whole family.

Sinanda had worked hard and had done well. He had become an officer. When he was in his late twenties, although he was not popular with his men, he had risen to the rank of colonel in charge of a regiment. But now Sinanda was not just thinking of providing enough money for the family. Sinanda had had much bigger plans.

Two days after his twenty-ninth birthday, Sinanda seized power from the reigning king, Fernando the Third, and became king of Mamanga in his place. Fernando was an old man, and the army was tired of him. In the last three years he had spent less and less money on the army and other things in Bamanga and more and more on his great houses and on his wives and relatives.

When Sinanda had plotted with the other officers to become king, he had promised that he would make the army the most important thing in Bamanga again. Some officers had eagerly agreed to support him. On the night of the rebellion, he and the other officers had attacked the palace with Sinanda's regiment and three other regiments. The soldiers in the palace had not surrendered quickly. There was a long fight before Colonel Sinanda captured the buildings.

Sinanda had declared himself king and had moved into the palace at once, taking his wife Mirama and his son Danta with him.

That afternoon all the leaders in the country came and promised to support him. With the army helping Sinanda there was very little they could do.

Sinanda found the palace more beautiful than anything he had ever seen. It was a dream come true. It had every luxury you could wish for. No African King had ever lived in such a luxurious palace.

On his first night there, Sinanda slept very deeply. Queen Mirama had to shake him to waken him the next morning.

'Wake up! Wake up!' she said. "It's morning.'

Golden rays of sunshine poured into the bedroom.

'What time is it?' Sinanda asked.

'It's eight o'clock. You have you first appointment at nine.'

'Hmmm ... it can wait! A man must rest. I am the king now. Let me first enjoy this marvellous palace, this soft bed, those fine paintings of the walls.'

Sinanda lay for a while. Then he got out of bed, walked to the window and peered out at the new day.

For the first few months Sinanda worked quite hard. He was always lazy, but now he seemed to try harder. He did some of the things he knew a good king would do. But this work did not last very long. He enjoyed being king. He did not want to work. He loved the beautiful palace and the swimming pool. He loved to play soccer and walk in the palace grounds. But he also worried that others might want to become king in his place.

2

It was a year since Sinanda had become king of Bamanga. During that time, he had started to change. Queen Mirama had tried to make everything happy for him, but Sinanda was suspicious of everyone. He had also become very cruel.

This morning Queen Mirama had laid out a breakfast of Bamanga river fish, scrambled eggs, freshly ground coffee, fresh bread and goat's cheese. The smell of the coffee brought Sinanda to the table.

His son Danta and Queen Mirama were already helping themselves to the food. Sinanda sat down, but before he could start to eat, he suddenly sprang up.

'I must go now,' he said, and left the table and hurried out of the room.

It seemed that he could not sit still for more than a few moments. He walked through the palace grounds until he came to the soccer pitch he had built. Sinanda liked to watch soccer and sometimes he played in the royal team.

Everyone knew that Sinanda had to win. The captain of the opposing team could spend some time in prison if the king's side was defeated.

He came to the great wall around the palace grounds and stopped at the orchard. The orchard produced golden oranges, Indian mangoes, and huge grapes. Sinanda had flown grape seedlings into Bamanga from France.

He employed French gardeners and winemakers. Their job was to turn the grapes into wine for Sinanda's dining table. King Sinanda never drank any other wine. He was afraid of being poisoned.

Danta came running after him, and soon, Queen Mirama joined them.

'Danta, it's time for school,' she said.

Danta made a face. He was never allowed outside the palace now. His teachers had been brought from another country and came to the palace every day to teach him. His playmates were searched at the gate before being allowed into the palace to play with him.

'He can go to school in half an hour,' King Sinanda said.

Danta excitedly pointed out the huge oranges and Indian mangoes, but he did not touch them. No one was ever permitted to pick any of the ripe fruit. If they did, the king would quickly be told and the punishment would be a terrible beating, or even worse.

Danta took his father's hand. They walked to the other end of the palace gardens. Here was the king's zoo. The air was filled with the sounds of strange birds from the Amazon River in South America and the forests of India and China. There were animals from all over Africa and Asia. The zoo was so big it was really a kind of game park. No one in Bamanga was allowed to see it.

They had stopped in front of the lions' cage. The king called to one of the attendants. The man immediately seized one of the dogs that were running around and threw it to the lions. The king stood watching as the lions ate the screaming animal. Then he roared with laughter.

'That's how I shall finish all my enemies,' he said.

The next morning, the king lay in bed until late again. He lay until late most mornings now. Then he got up and walked to the balcony of his bedroom. He stood gazing at all the splendour. He turned to the queen, who was waiting for him to come to breakfast.

'Mirama, this is the most wonderful palace. I don't want to live anywhere else,' he said.

'As you wish,' Queen Mirama replied.

'Why do you speak that way? Don't you like it here?' King Sinanda's eyes glowed with anger.

'I do,' said the queen, 'but–'

'But what?'

'Never mind,' said the queen.

Danta looked from his father to his mother and

was afraid. He did not like to see his father angry with his mother.

When he was alone with the queen, Danta questioned his mother.

'Why did my father look at you like that?'

'Look at me ... like what?'

'Like he was going to hit you. Like he was very angry with you.'

'Really?' said the queen. 'I did not notice.'

Danta said, 'When he asked you how you like the palace, you did not praise it–'

He stopped suddenly. He saw the tears filling his mother's eyes and running down her cheeks.

'You are my son,' she said. 'Soon you will be a man. You may want to be a soldier.' She paused. 'I don't know what happens to men when they become soldiers. Your father is always wanting to destroy ... When will it end?'

She wiped away her tears and cleaned her face. 'Let us go for a walk,' she said. 'I worry too much. I am upset.'

'Don't be upset again, Mother,' said Danta. 'I don't like to see you cry.'

'Let us walk. Then we can sit. I will tell you about Bamanga and why I am worried.'

3

'In the old days,' said Queen Mirama when they were seated, 'Bamanga was ruled by the family of King Fernando.'

Danta listened to his mother, his hands on his chin.

'At that time, at the time of Fernando the First, there were no white men or any other strangers in Bamanga. Only the Bamanga people lived here. We did not meet people from the outside world.'

'You mean we had no visitors at all?' asked Danta.

'Just people living near us. We always had plenty to live on. Some of our people went to sea to fish in their canoes. Others were farmers. There was fish and meat and milk, and we cut down the palm fruit from the palm trees. Then one day the white traders arrived from Europe. First there were the Spanish people. Then the Portuguese. The French came, and the English. They fought among themselves for the trade with Bamanga. They taught us to fight. They taught some of our men to be soldiers instead of fishermen and farmers.

'The white men gave Fernando the first guns and whisky and he gave them land to build on. Then they bought slaves. We sold them slaves. They took the slaves to America and to the West Indies to work in the plantations.'

'What happened after that?' asked Danta, fascinated by his mother's story.

'More traders came. They bought palm oil. They shipped it away to Europe in special boats called tankers—just like they ship crude oil today. Still other white men came. King Fernando agreed to buy things from them and to sell things to them. They built churches and schools and trading posts. But some of them brought guns and soldiers and they conquered Bamanga.

'Fernando the Second was still king, but he ruled under the European government. Bamanga was now a British colony. The colonial government made many of our people join the army. The people of Bamanga were forced to join the army of Bamanga, and they had to fight the wars of the European government.

'In 1941, the soldiers of Bamanga were taken to India and Burma to fight in the white man's army. Many never returned. Your father wasn't even born then. But his people—the Timanga people, where your grandmother and grandfather come from—were nothing. They were not important. They were just a small group in the middle of Bamanga.'

'Why was that?' asked Danta.

'In Bamanga it was like this: the Gammans were the rulers. King Fernando's family was Gamman. The Gammans were mostly Muslim. Some of them spoke Arabic. They lived in the north of Bamanga, but they came south to rule. They were the most ambitious of the peoples in Bamanga. They wanted to organize the country.

"Then there were the Managas. They were mostly traders. They travelled far and wide in Africa to buy and sell, and they were Christians. A few of them were Muslims, but even those went to school to study commerce. The banks in Bamanga today are run by the Managas. Also, the big industries. Some Managas even started to assemble motor cars.'

'But, Mother, why are you telling me all this?'

'So that you will understand what is happening and where you come from ... It is my duty to tell you, my son.'

'What happened to the Managas?' asked Danta.

'They still live here in Bamanga,' said his mother. 'But what you must know is this. The Managas and the Bamans and the Timangans were nothing. The Gammans ruled us almost as cruelly as the European government did. I come from Bama in the eastern part of Bamanga. Our people love technology. We can build anything with metal or wood – and it works. The Gammans used my people in the factories and industries. But one of the good things your father did at first was to make sure that they paid the other peoples a proper wage. After years and years of rule by the Gammans your father started to change things.'

'How?' asked Danta, in amazement.

'As you know, your father comes from Timanga. His family is poor. The people of Timanga were nothing. But many of them, and many Bamans too, joined the army. Everybody had grown tired of Fernando, even the young Gammans in the army. You see, after Fernando the First died, Fernando the Second became king. He was even worse than the old Fernando. Then Bamanga got her independence. Fernando the Third led the people to Independence, but he was even more wicked than all the others. He stole money and stored it away in banks overseas. He built palaces for himself all over the country. And all the time the people were suffering.'

'My father and the soldiers killed him when they took over the palace, didn't they?' asked Danta.

'I do not know,' said Queen Mirama sadly. 'No one ever saw him again. But your father started to make things better. Until now. Now he is frightened all the time. He feels he must kill to protect us.'

'Mother, I want to go away. The soldiers will kill me too.'

Queen Mirama looked at her son in surprise. 'Don't talk like that. You wouldn't want to leave your mother here all alone, would you?'

'But, Mother, it's true. I read in a book where bad men kidnapped a king's son and – '

'That's only a story,' his mother said, trying to calm him.

'But why do soldiers always want to rule?' Danta asked fearfully.

'Because they want to tell people what to do. People fear a ruler. He's like a god. He can put people in prison. He can spend money as he likes on anything he likes. He can command armies to go to war. He can, he can, play the tough guy.' Mirama smiled at her own words.

Danta laughed. 'I like that.'

'What?'

'Playing the tough guy.'

'Playing the tough guy makes people suffer. Many die. Many have to run away as refugees. It is very sad.'

'Is Bamanga going to be a bad place?' Danta asked in a frightened voice.

'If they continue to fight your father, it will become bad. The people will suffer.'

'Tell Father to stop killing people!' Danta said.

'I have tried to stop him,' Queen Mirama said with tears in her eyes. 'But he says it is kill or be killed.'

'That is terrible,' her son said. He shivered as if it had suddenly become very cold.

4

Sinanda was Timangan. He came from a small group of people living in central Bamanga. All the other groups were larger in number than the Timangans. For years, the Timangans had been attacked and treated very badly.

The Timangans were a warlike people but, until Sinanda rose to power, they had no real leadership. Over the years, they had joined the Bamangan army in their thousands. But even when Sinanda became a colonel. Very few had become sergeants and only one or two Timangans had become officers. People from the other groups who joined the army also did the jobs they were good at. The Gamman government appointed Gammans as commanders and officers. The Managas ran the administration, and the Bamans were to be found in the workshops and technical services.

When Sinanda became king, he retired many of the officers and men from the other groups. He got rid of many of the Gammans and the Managas. Most of the people did not think there was anything wrong with this.

Bamanga had been ruled for over a hundred years by the Gammans. The country was still poor and the only people who seemed to benefit from Gamman rule were the Gammans. The last Gamman king was to be Fernando the Third.

When Sinanda realised that he was feared and respected by both the other officers and the men, he began to plot the overthrow of Fernando the Third. He held secret meetings with officers he could trust. Slowly he persuaded more and more of them that it would be good for everyone in the country if Fernando was deposed and Sinanda became king.

Finally, Sinanda had gathered together a battalion of officers and men he could trust. Most of them were Timingan, although there were some Managas and Bamans. They agreed that they would have storm the palace and capture Fernando. He would not give up the throne any other way.

Sinanda moved his men until they were all placed in two barracks near the palace. One night, when everyone slept, the battalions attacked the palace. Fernandos men fought more bravely than Sinanda had expected, and the palace was heavily fortified. The fighting went on all the night and most of the next day. Dozens of soldiers on both sides were killed in the line of defence and the palace was theirs.

They found Fernando hiding under a huge table

in one of the cellars. One of Sinanda's special service units took him into the forests of Bamanga. He had never been heard of since.

After the overthrow of Fernando the Third, Sinanda began his reign as if he meant to improve the country and give everyone a better chance to have a good life. Since he had no royal blood in his veins, the people of Bamanga believed that he would understand their difficulties and try to make them happy.

In his first speech to the people of Bamanga he said, 'People of Bamanga! The tyrant Fernando has been overthrown! There will be no more suffering ... no more unemployment. Every man will be able to buy meat and a measure of rice to feed his family. When Fernando was king, you could not afford to take your children to school ... The teachers were not paid their salaries ... We will change all this. There will be no more oppression ... There will be no more oppression of Timangans.

'Bamanga belongs to all of us – Timangans, Managas, Bamans and Gammans. Good people of Bamanga, the future belongs to all of us. What we decide to do is up to us. I promise you a happier life, more food, more clean water, more education, more everything. I will stop now. I am not a man of many words.' Few people there realised that Sinanda had grown bored with the speech.

The people cheered happily and threw hits, sticks and anything else they could find into the air. They marched through the streets, singing and waving the flag of Bamanga. 'Down with tyrants! Long live Sinanda!'

'Now,' they said, 'now we can enjoy life.'

But it was not long before Sinanda began to forget all about his promises. At first, he only laughed when he heard that his people were still suffering. He did not care if many Bamangans could not even afford one meal a day. Soon he became angry if anyone mentioned suffering and shortages.

It grew worse. Anyone who complained of hardship was taken away by drunken soldiers and was never heard of again.

Now Sinanda started to make changes in the country. The first thing he did was to dismiss everyone from the public service and the government who was not a Timangan. The old government ministers were sacked and all the new ones came from Timanga. The Chief of Police and all the regional commanders were Timangan.

He closed the parliament buildings and appointed a new cabinet to help him run the country. All the members were Timangan. All his personal staff came from Timanga – cooks, stewards, drivers, gatekeepers.

'When I surround myself with my own people, I feel safer,' he said.

Sinanda now started a campaign of terror against all the men who had served Fernando the Third. He arranged for the kidnapping and killing of the Chief Justice of Bamanga and all the other judges. Senior army officers disappeared, never to be seen again. Managing directors and leaders of business disappeared or were found dead in their cars or houses. The killings went on and on. Nothing seemed to satisfy Sinanda except more blood.

5

Like most soldiers and people who have not been very well educated, Sinanda was very superstitious. He asked the advice of medicine men before he made any important decisions. He also believed in ghosts. He knew what had happened to Fernando the Third. He was terrified that Fernando's ghost would haunt him.

In order to protect himself, Sinanda surrounded himself with witch doctors, prophets, fortune-tellers, praise singers and even palace clowns. He blamed and punished these people for anything that happened.

The medicine men and the clowns waited anxiously for the king's summons. He might call them at any time during the night or day. He might suddenly wake up in bed after a nightmare. He would send Mirama to call one of the witch doctors to give him something to make him sleep peacefully or to explain the meaning of the nightmare.

Although the king had many such advisers, the wisest of them was a man called Mamazda. Sinanda knew this and he consulted Mamazda every day.

Several times during the last few months Sinanda had talked to Mamazda about the dangers facing him and the possible threats to his throne. Sinanda knew he had enemies. He killed as many of them as he could, but he seemed to find more and more enemies everywhere he looked.

He had looked at Mamazda and said, 'I want to be king forever. I want you to use your magic to make me king forever.'

Then he had waved his hand for Mamazda to leave the room.

A week later the king summoned Mamazda to another meeting. Mamazda collected all his fortuneteller's tools and hurried to the palace. He was taken to a secret room where the king was sitting on a low stool.

Mamazda carefully brushed clean a space on the carpeted floor. Then he spread a mat of very soft reeds on the floor. He poured very fine white sand on to the mat. The sand had been collected from the bed of the river Bamanga on the first night after a full moon and then specially sifted. Secret spells were spoken to make the magic in the sand more powerful.

Mamazda spread and smoothed the sand with the edge of his right hand and then made patterns in it. He gazed at the patterns. At the same time, he put pinches of snuff on to the back of his hand and sniffed them deeply. He sat for a long time as if in a trance.

'Well?' Sinanda said at last. His voice was hoarse with excitement and his eyes were glaring at Mamazda.

'If you want to be king forever –' said Mamazda.

'I want! I want to be king forever! I must be king forever! Nobody shall succeed me ... if I die, Bamanga dies with me ...' The king's voice trembled as he spoke.

Mamazda gave him a curious look but said nothing.

Sinanda began to shout. 'Without me there must be no Bamanga. Do you hear?'

His eyes flashed angrily, and he brought his hands together with a loud crack.

'Your wish shall come true, O King – but there is a price to pay.'

'A price? Tell me, what price must the king pay?'

Mamazda heard the warning tone in the king's voice, but he went on almost desperately.

'There is always a price to pay if you ask the gods for help. And in this case, there is no other way. The sand tells me we need the gods to help us. We must pay their price.'

He stopped for a moment and tried to think clearly. The king was becoming angrier and angrier. Mamazda was more and more frightened, but he had to go on. He knows there was only one way to make sure the king stayed alive.

'What you wish will come true ... but you must sacrifice ...' Mamazda paused again. 'You must sacrifice something dear to you.'

Sinanda jumped up in a rage.

Mamazda lay on the floor in terror, raising his hands to try to protect himself. 'No! No! No! Not that. Not your son,' he shouted in fear. 'No, if Your Majesty wanted money, the gods might ask for his first-born son and heir as a sacrifice. But Your Majesty does not want money. What you are asking for is much much more than money. What you want is eternal power and more power. To be like one of the gods themselves!'

'Get to the point!' Sinanda shouted. 'What are you telling me?'

Mamazda was a brave man. He was a great witch doctor and there was very little that he feared. But he did fear the terrible anger of the king. He rose to his knees again and began to make patterns in the sand. He smoothed them out and made more. Then he took the king's had and presses it into the sand. He began to recite strange words in a low voice. His chant rose almost to a shout. Suddenly he stopped.

A frown appeared on his face. 'Your Majesty, your wish shall come true, if –'

'If what?' Sinanda shouted. 'Tell me, you idiot!'

Mamazda felt anger in his heart. A witch doctor should be respected. It was bad to call a great medicine man an idiot. But Mamazda hid his anger and pointed at the patterns.

He began to trace the message of the spirits. His body started to shake as if he had a high fever. His voice seemed to come from beyond his body.

'I read what I see! The gods have spoken! You can

rule forever if that is your desire. The gods have spoken. If you want to rule forever, you must never, never leave the palace or go outside the palace grounds again.'

Sinanda stood quite still. For a long time the full meaning did not seem to strike him. Then suddenly he drew himself up to his full height.

'Rubbish!' he shouted. 'Nonsense and rubbish!'

'That is what you must do–if you want to be king forever.' Mamazda shook his head. 'I have told you everything.'

'Rubbish!' repeated Sinanda. 'It is impossible! Not to leave the palace! Me! Sinanda. A prisoner?' He began to laugh and slap his thigh.

'Your Majesty, your wish shall come true, it ...'

Many people said that it was not a good sign when he laughed like this. Mamazda became frightened as he watched Sinanda rolling about in laughter.

'It is not a thing to laugh at,' Mamazda said nervously. 'You are a civilised king. You do not need to leave the palace. You can listen to the radio. You can speak on the radio, and everyone will hear you. You have the telephone. You have commanders and officers, assistants and servants. They can carry out your every wish and command ...'

'It's not the same thing,' shouted Sinanda, still laughing. 'It's not the same thing.'

'You have to learn to trust people–'

'Trust? I trust nobody, you hear me? Sinanda trusts nobody!'

'You cannot do it all alone.' Mamazda pleaded with the king.

'I don't care. There is nobody in the whole world I can trust with anything. Do you think I could trust anyone with my life?'

Mamazda was a patient man. 'But–just think, O King! You need people!'

'Aha!' said Sinanda. His eyes were blazing with rage now. 'Now I understand. The servant wants to be master. Why don't you try to become king, Mamazda? Why don't you become king of Bamanga ... eh? I see now that's what you want!'

'Your Majesty–I am happy to be a medicine man. I do not want to be king. I believe I know my job well–'

'How dare you speak to King Sinanda like that!'

'Dear King, the truth is not always easy. Sometimes, it is very bitter. If it is lies and sweet words you want–do not send for Mamazda!' Mamazda's courage had returned. He knew he was in terrible danger. He knew his life hung by a thread, but a great witch doctor had to defend himself even against evil kings.

'Enough!' shouted the king. 'Go!'

Mamazda quickly picked up his things from the floor. He rolled his mat and corked his snuff bottle. He did not see a piece of cloth he had left on the ground. He did see the wicked gleam in the king's eyes, and he trembled inwardly. Outwardly, he remained calm.

'Your Majesty, if you accept the offer of the gods, please remember this. Never step outside the palace grounds again. If you do, you will surely die.'

'Go! Go!' screamed Sinanda. 'Get out of my sight!'

Sinanda seemed about to rush upon the witch doctor and strike him.

Mamazda cowered where he was. All the evil stories he heard about the king came rushing into his mind. That he was a killer! That he hated to be told the truth if it was unpleasant. That if he was in a rage, he would attack people like a madman. That he was a man who surrounded himself with liars and favourites. They were all men who would tell him what he wanted to hear – that he was the greatest man in Bamanga, and the greatest king on Earth.

When Mamazda had collected all his medicines, he slowly began to leave the palace.

But in his secret room, Sinanda's anger grew until he almost burst. He walked to and from muttering to himself.

'If there is a parade in town, I cannot go wearing my medals ... If there is a reception, I cannot attend it. He's telling me I must remain here in the palace! Me! Sinanda!'

He burst out again in a long, wicked laugh. It was a laugh that did not touch his eyes. It was a laugh that sounded like Mamazda's death song.

6

King Sinanda felt that Mamazda had betrayed him. How could his favourite witch doctor say those things to him? He had given him everything and this was how he behaved.

'He's mad! Mamazda is mad! I have no use for madmen ... I have no use for men who want to destroy the king ...Yes! He wants to destroy the king!'

Sinanda rushed to his office holding Mamazda's piece of cloth. He pressed a button. In a few moments his Chief Security Officer, a gorilla-like man called Garanga, hobbled in. Garanga was a Timangan and he was a loyal supporter of Sinanda. He had been wounded in the attack of the palace the night Fernando the Third had been overthrown. For this reason Sinanda felt he could be trusted and so he made him his Head of Palace Security.

'Garanga!'

Garanga stood as close to attention as his wounded leg would permit. He had a huge barrel chest, bowed legs, made worse by his injury, and a great scowling face. People said he loved to hurt things. They also said that his red eyes were the result of smoking drug-filled cigarettes. Whatever they were, they had a foul smell which seemed to hang around Garanga in a cloud.

'Your Majesty, sah!' Garanga shouted, and he tried even harder to stand to attention.

'Mamazda!' said the king, with a strange look in his eyes. He pointed in the direction of the witch doctor who was walking down the path to the palace gates.

Garanga hated Mamazda, because the king liked and listened to what he had to say.

'Mamazda, Your Majesty,' said Garanga, a cruel look on his great face. 'Giving trouble?'

'He wants to put me in prison,' said the king.

'What?' shouted Garanga, the look on his face becoming more cruel by the minute.

'He wants to lock me up forever.'

'He's mad!' Garanga stamped about like a gorilla in a cage.

As they spoke a door behind Sinanda's desk opened. Queen Mirama started to come in. She saw Garanga and stopped. He frightened her more than anyone she knew. Except maybe Sinanda when he was in one of his terrible moods.

'Is there anything wrong, O King?' she asked.

'Mamazda wants me to spend the rest of my life in prison.'

'Are you sure, O King?'

'Mamazda claims he saw a sign ... from the spirits. If I want to be king forever, I must never leave the palace grounds again.'

'The king must rule forever,' shouted Garanga, nearly coming to attention again.

'Be calm,' Mirama said. 'I believe Mamazda. What the spirits have told him may be true. You do have enemies. You have told me so yourself. You've told me this is the reason why so many people have been killed or disappeared. Better listen to him ...'

Mirama suddenly stopped talking. She had noticed that Garanga and the king were exchanging glances. She remembered the rumour that whenever the king summoned Garanga, somebody usually died.

She quickly left the room.

Danta met her in the corridor. 'Is Father angry again?'

At first Mirama did not answer. Then she explained what had happened.

Danta said, 'Mother, can't you stop them?'

'I tried,' replied the queen. She walked slowly towards her room.

The king paid no attention to Mirama's fears. Instead he fixed Garanga with a long steady look. Garanga read the message in the depths of the king's eyes and understood. He knew what he must do. The king handed him Mamazda's piece of cloth.

Garanga hurried out and shouted for the soldier in charge of the dog kennels. He quickly ordered him to bring Rawoulf, the killer dog. He gave the dog the piece of cloth to smell. Then he unleashed the semi-wild beast.

The half-dog, half-wolf smelled the ground for a moment. Then it smelled the air. It leapt along the path after the witch doctor. Mamazda had gone halfway to the palace gates. He turned when he heard the snarling animal behind him. He almost fell over in terror. He turned again and ran on. He looked desperately for something to defend himself with. He could see nothing.

No matter how fast he ran the beast quickly caught up with him. Now it was snapping at his heels. Then it was snapping at the back of his neck. The great animal knocked him to the ground. Within moments it was tearing out his throat.

'Idiot!' muttered Garanga, who had watched with a look of satisfaction on his face. 'Look what's happened to the king's favourite!'

7

Sinanda was born in a tiny village fifty kilometres from Tima, which was the only town in Timanga. He had three brothers and two sisters. He was the youngest of the six children.

His father and mother could not afford to send all the children to school, so only the two oldest boys received a proper education. His mother tried to make sure that all the children could read and write a little. Sinanda was not a very intelligent boy, but he was not stupid. He wanted to do well and make plenty of money. But he wanted it at once. He was greedy, but he did not want to work hard. He had worked hard to learn what his mother could teach him. He had only done this because everyone told him that education was important.

Sinanda, like all the other boys in the village, had to work every day. He and his sisters collected water every morning at daybreak. Immediately after a breakfast of akara and tea, he went with the village boys. Their job was to drive the goats and cattle into the bush to look for good grass and fresh leaves.

The animals belonged to the various families in the village. Sinanda's father owned ten goats and four cows. The cows gave them all the milk they needed. Compared to most of the other men in the village, Sinanda's father was quite rich. But they had had a bad harvest the previous year and Pa Mininda, Sinanda's father, had borrowed money from the wealthiest man in the village. Pa Mininda was hoping for a good harvest this year, or he would have to sell some of the animals to pay back the money.

Sinanda was not popular with the other boys. He was very big for his age and very strong. He liked to bully the smaller boys and make them do all the work. He would lie on a pile of grass while the other boys looked after the animals. At first, some of the other boys flattered him and pretended to be his friend. But soon they grew tired of his bullying. One day, they all ganged up on him and gave him a severe beating. He was so badly beaten he had to stay in bed for three days. His mother, who could see no wrong with her son, blamed everyone but Sinanda.

After that, Sinanda worked along with the other boys, but he hated them in his heart.

When he was fourteen, he read a poster in the village asking for recruits to join the Royal Bamangan Army. Sinanda wanted to get away from the village. But there was one problem. Applicants had to be at least fifteen years of age when they applied. Sinanda read the words carefully. There was free food and accommodation, free uniforms, free education for those who wanted to study, and recruits would receive a weekly wage.

At that moment Sinanda decided to join the army on his fifteenth birthday. He went to talk to his mother. He recited all the things he had seen on the poster. He told her that he would work hard and really make something of himself.

There was nothing in the village for him, and all the other boys were jealous of him, he said. When he was successful, he would bring his father and mother to live with him in Port Bamanga. He did not intend to spend money on his mother and father, but it sounded good to say it.

His mother knew the other children in the village did not like him, but Sinanda was her favourite. She was sure he could be an important person. She said she would talk to his father. Pa Mininda was very worried about money and the harvest. He did not listen carefully to what his wife told him. What he did hear was very good. It would help him a lot if there was one less mouth to feed. It would help if Sinanda sent some of his wages each week. He agreed to let Sinanda join the army.

The nine months to Sinanda's fifteenth birthday seemed to pass more and more slowly. Sinanda's head was full of the army. He marched everywhere. He saluted the village headman and the witch doctor.

He saluted the wealthy man who had worked for years in Port Bamanga. This was the man who had lent Sinanda's father the money to buy grain for this year's crop.

He tried to get the other boys to play soldiers with him. After one game in which he hurt four of them with a big stick, no one would play with him again.

Six months before his fifteenth birthday, Sinanda and his mother wrote to the army headquarters in Port Bamanga. Two weeks later one of the women in the village told him that there was a letter for him at the village post office. It was an application form to join the army. It had to be completed in Sinanda's own handwriting and signed by his father and the village headman. Sinanda sent the form off immediately.

One month before his fifteenth birthday he received another letter. This time he had to go to the army barracks in Tima for an interview and a medical examination.

Although he was very nervous, Sinanda enjoyed every minute of his visit to Tima. He had never seen a town before, and he stared in amazement at the shops and buildings. He had come with his father, who was required to attend the interview and sign all the papers for Sinanda's entry into the army.

Sinanda tried even harder to look like a soldier as they approached the gates of the army barracks. He put his shoulders back and marched alongside his father feeling proud of himself. The interview was very short and the officer in charge was clearly impressed by Sinanda's height and size and his enthusiasm. After the medical examination, the officer told Sinanda that he would hear if his application had been successful within a few weeks.

Sinanda returned home full of his trip to Tima. He told anyone who would listen all about it. He exaggerated some of the story, saying how the army liked him. Also, he said they had told him he would be an officer in no time at all.

Two months passed and Sinanda began to believe that the army had not accepted him. The other boys began to laugh behind his back. They pretended to march the way he did, and they called each other captain and general and they saluted every time they saw him.

Just when Sinanda was about to burst with rage, his father came home from the village ship one evening with a thick envelope. He was to report to the army barracks in Tima in seven days. He would be taken to Port Bamanga to begin his army training. There was a list of things he had to bring with him, and two more forms to be filled in and signed. The most important one had to be signed by both Sinanda and his father. It said that Sinanda agreed to remain in the army for a period of twenty-two years. He could, if the army was satisfied with him, sign for a further twenty-two years at the end of the first period.

The morning on which Sinanda left the village was the happiest day of his life and the bus that took him to Tima was better than any magic carpet. He said goodbye to his mother and father and brothers and sisters as quickly as he could. Then he loaded his box on to the bus and scrambled in after it. he waved at his family and settled down in his seat. He would show everyone what he could do.

8

Shortly after Sinanda became king, he brought his father and mother to Port Bamanga to live in the palace with him. He had given them a magnificent guest house with servants and a motor car to take them wherever they wanted to go.

At first they had been proud of their son and all the things he said he was going to do. But they became worried when they saw his terrible rages and heard the stories about the killings and the disappearances. They missed the village life. They missed their sons and daughters and the villagers. They even missed working on the farm every day. Worst of all people in the streets booed and hissed at them when they went out in the car. They felt that they had become prisoners in their son's palace.

After a long discussion they decided to talk to Sinanda. It was late at night, but they went to the palace and asked to see their son. They were told he had gone to bed, but they demanded to see him.

The king finally appeared, dressed in his army uniform.

'Well?' he asked. 'What's so urgent? Is anything the matter?'

'Don't be angry with us, son. We have come to tell you something.'

'What?'

'We do not want to live in this palace anymore.'

'Why?' asked Sinanda, starting to get angry.

'We're afraid,' his father said.

'We want to go back to our village in Timanga,' said his mother. 'Do not forget, your father and mother are poor people. We are used to being poor ...'

The words drove Sinanda into a furious temper. He began to pace up and down the room. For a moment he forgot he was standing before his parents, and he began to shout. He got more and more angry when he saw the tears in his mother's eyes.

'So!' he shouted. 'You are not on my side? You are against me. You do not want me to be king. Everybody in Bamanga fears me! Everybody in Bamangs respects me! Everybody in Bamanga loves me – everybody but you!' He pointed at his mother.

His father could not allow his son to speak this way. But he did not know what to do. Sinanda's rage frightened him. He tried to explain as gently as he could.

'You are wrong, my son. Of course we love you,' he said. 'We love you and wish you well – but we do not enjoy this kind of life. It is not for us.'

The noise was so great that Danta was wakened

from his sleep. He crept along the corridor and peered in through a crack in the door. When he saw his father shouting at his grandmother and grandfather, he ran quickly back to his room and locked the door. He beat his fists against his pillows. But the shouts still came to his ears.

Sinanda was almost screaming with rage now.

'I've brought you from the village,' shouted Sinanda. 'I've given you a lovely house. You can go anywhere you want in your motor car. I've given you every comfort. What do you want?' The king stared at them with a mad look in his eyes.

Sinanda terrified his mother, but she spoke up bravely. 'It's not comfort we want, son, but peace! The people of Bamanga are dying.'

She was going to say more, but Pa Mininda spoke quickly to stop her.

'We're not used to so much luxury and comfort, my son,' he said. 'We're afraid.'

Sinanda screamed and screamed at his mother and father until they nearly melted with fear.

'You don't have to work! You don't even have to go to the shops! You don't have to do anything! You can just sit and enjoy your –'

'No, no!' his father interrupted him. 'We are bored ... We want to go back and work on the farm again. We miss the farm. We miss our neighbours. We are used to farming and labouring. This life is not good for us.'

Sinanda looked at his parents. He had stopped screaming now. Instead, he began to plead with them.

'I beg you to stay ... It will be a disgrace for me if you leave me like this.' He held his arms out to them. 'I have become king of Bamanga. The father of the king cannot farm! It is poor man's work.'

'But,' said his father, 'you are always telling the people on the radio – farm, farm, farm ... I heard you again today. I am one of those people. My son, let me go and farm. People will see that your father is a farmer, and you will be proud of that. Your people will be proud of you.'

Sinanda stared at his father. His eyes slowly grew angry again.

'Oh, demons!' cried the king. His face had an evil look, and he rubbed his hands together as if washing them. 'Save me from these demons!' He started to pull at his hair in his rage. 'So you are against me – you too?'

His father's eyes grew dull with fear.

Sinanda suddenly went quiet again. He sat, holding his head in his hands. When he raised his head again, his eyes were flaming with rage. 'I shall have to arrange a special car for you ... Yes, I shall have to –'

At that moment Queen Mirama appeared beside him. She had changed over the months. In an attempt to please the king, she had bought many new clothes. Now she wore a beautiful green sleeping gown, and she smelt of an expensive perfume. She looked more beautiful than ever.

'I heard what they said, dear king,' She smiled at him and placed her hand on his shoulder. 'They don't like the palace. But surely they won't leave us now? I don't understand this ... It is a very bad sign! Something bad will happen!'

King Sinanda said nothing. He sat staring at his parents with the same evil look in his eyes.

'Why don't you stop them?' Queen Mirama turned to her husband. 'This will be a disgrace. What will people say?'

Still King Sinanda said nothing. He stared at his mother and father who were sitting nervously holding hands.

'Very well! Let them go!' Mirama said sadly. 'If they want to go, let them go.' She began to sob. 'If they want to disgrace the king ...'

Sinanda stood up. He looked at his father and mother again.

'I have asked you to stay with us, to show that you are proud of me.' He spoke quite calmly now. 'If you cannot stay ...'

He turned to leave the room. His mother came after him.

'So we can go?' she asked. 'Oh, thank you, thank you ... God bless you.' She fell to her knees. 'God will bless you, my son.'

Pa Mininda and his wife returned to their guest house. They were too tired to sleep. They lay on their bed and made plans for the future.

The next morning Sinanda came to see them. He was calm and even smiled a little. He asked them again to stay in Port Bamanga at the palace. They told him they still wanted to return to Timanga.

They were frightened. They did not want him to go into another rage. But Sinanda only smiled.

'If that is your decision, I will not try to change it,' he said.

'God bless you, my son,' Pa Mininda said. 'Your mother and I thank you for all this, but we will be happier in the village. With all the people we know.'

'Very well,' said the king. 'The car will be ready to take you to Timanga tomorrow at down. Pack all your things and have them ready.'

He put his arms around them both for a moment and then left the room.

The next morning, they set off in the early dawn. There had been more tears from Queen Mirama, but King Sinanda said goodbye with a smile. He waved until the car was out of the palace gates.

They drove for four hours along the highway going north. The driver stopped and poured them tea from a flask. He said that he was a little worried about the brakes. They were not working very well. But Pa Mininda was eager to get home to the village. He asked the driver to drive on. They stopped later at an army base for more petrol. The driver asked the mechanic to check the brakes for him. They could find nothing wrong.

It was late afternoon. The highway stopped at Tima. They were now driving along a dirt road about an hour from the village.

Sinanda's mother was sleeping, giving little snores from time to time. Pa Mininda shook her gently. She opened her eyes and looked about her.

'Where are we?' she asked.

'Quite near the village.'

'Ah, now I am happy! I feel free now!'

The car bounced along the poor road. The driver was trying to go as quickly as possible. He wanted to get his passengers home and be back on the road to Port Bamanga.

'Just Bujama Hill, the bridge over the river and we are nearly home,' said Pa Mininda.

The car started down the long, steep hill. The driver braked to slow the car. The brakes did not seem to work. He pumped the brakes harder. The car still did not slow down. It was going faster and faster now. The driver tried hard to keep the car on the track. At the bottom of the hill, the road curved round and crossed a bridge over the river. As they neared the bottom, the driver pulled at the steering wheel to try to get round the bend. The car was going far too fast. It began to turn over. It turned over once and then again. Everyone in the car was thrown heavily from the floor to roof. The car was now turning over again and again. Finally, it crashed through the bridge and down into the river below.

One of the boys from the village saw the accident.

He ran to get help and all the villagers rushed to drag Pa Mininda and his wife from the car. There seemed to be blood everywhere.

It took many hours for the ambulance to reach the village and many more hours before Sinanda's mother and father reached the hospital. Long before then, both parents had stopped breathing.

Sinanda did not come to the funeral in the village. He sent an army general instead.

At the funeral many people said that it had been an accident. Sinanda could never kill his parents they said. No matter how much he loved power.

But there were many more who whispered that Sinanda was an evil man. He had offered his parents as a sacrifice to the devils he worshiped. A sacrifice so that he might rule forever.

9

From the moment Sinanda entered the army barracks in Tima, he was happy. He spent hours that first night looking at his uniforms, his boots, his physical training clothes, his rucksack, and all the other equipment he had been given. He went to the mirror to look at his haircut. His head gleamed in the light where they had shaved off all his hair. He lay on his bed and got up again. He turned on the taps and the showers. He washed his hands and dried them. He was happy.

Next morning at half past five, a bugle call wakened Sinanda and the other recruits from a deep sleep. A sergeant told them to put on their physical training clothes and get outside. They exercised and ran for an hour. Then they were told to shower and dress. They had half an hour to report for breakfast. Next they were given lessons in marching and going on parade. Then they had classroom instruction on how to use a rifle.

Sinanda learnt all the rules and regulations quickly. He was always first on parade. He was always the cleanest and neatest soldier. He tried to answer questions in the lessons before anyone else. He quickly made himself very unpopular with the other recruits. But Sinanda believed that they admired and respected him.

The officers watched all the recruits. They asked the sergeants about all the new soldiers. The sergeant in charge of Sinanda's platoon said they should make Sinanda a corporal. He was going to be a good soldier. He might even make a good sergeant someday. Sinanda was promoted to corporal next day. He was to be responsible for a group of men in the platoon.

Sinanda had made one friend in the army camp. He was another Timangan, from Tima, called Sikiwa. Sikiwa had joined the Royal Bamangan Army on the same day as Sinanda. They had travelled down to Poet Bamanga from Tima together. They had become friends almost by accident. Sikiwa had been made a corporal too, and they were in the same platoon. There was one difference. The men liked Sikiwa. They laughed with him and followed his orders quickly. Sinanda's men followed his orders because they were afraid of him.

After six months Sinanda's platoon completed their training. They were sent to the north-western border to help defend it against possible attacks. Fernando the Third hated the President of Rulindi, the neighbouring country, and both sides watched the frontier carefully. Also cattle rustlers often raided farms in northern Bamanga, and stole women and children as well as cattle.

'I'm hot and tired and dirty,' said Sinanda. 'What time is it?'

'It's twelve o'clock,' replied Sikiwa. 'Two more hours before we turn back.'

They were standing in the shade of a great mahogany tree. The rest of the platoon lay on the ground and drank water from their canteens or smoked cigarettes. They were patrolling thirty kilometres of border between the camp and the river Bamanga. They had seen nothing all day, except a few thin antelope and many hungry vultures. The lieutenant in charge of the platoon came over to them.

'I've a surprise for you,' he said. 'We have to make for the river and camp there for the night. The colonel is going to fly in by helicopter. We're going on a night patrol. On foot.'

'No beer tonight,' said Sikiwa. He laughed at the look on Sinanda's face. Sinanda always had a few beers on a Saturday night.

The noise of the helicopter wakened Sinanda who was sitting half asleep beside his rucksack. He called to the soldiers to get ready and then went with the lieutenant and Corporal Sikiwa to meet the colonel.

'We have some men who work on the other side of the border. One of them spotted a group of rustlers moving in this direction yesterday.' The colonel pointed to the map. Sinanda shone a torch on it to help them see clearly.

'We're here. We'll move north-west up the border and attack them as soon as they enter Bamanga, about here. One of the other platoons will move south-east to meet us. If we miss them, they should find them. All right? Well then, let's get started.'

It was all so quick, Sinanda never knew what happened. The platoon did not see the rustlers and the rustlers did not see the soldiers. One of the soldiers almost walked straight into the rustlers. The rustler fired his gun, and suddenly everyone was firing. Sinanda stopped beside the colonel and looked in amazement. A figure came out of the dark, pointed his rifle at the colonel, and fired. Sinanda tried to turn to get out of the way. His feet slipped and he fell directly in front of the colonel. The bullet struck him below the shoulder. Sinanda dropped unconscious to the ground.

The colonel fired his revolver at the rustler, but the figure had vanished into the darkness again. The colonel called for help. They quickly bandaged Sinanda and put him on a stretcher. The lieutenant ran up to report. He saw Sinanda on the stretcher.

'He saved my life,' the colonel said in a shaking

voice. 'He saw the gun and he threw himself in front of me. I've never seen anything like it. I didn't think Sinanda was a brave man, but he saved my life.'

Sinand woke up in the small hospital in the army camp. He quickly discovered that he had become a hero. A helicopter took him to Tima and then on to the big army hospital in Port Bamanga.

When he went back to his platoon three months later, Sergeant Sinanda wore a medal pinned to the left side of his chest.

10

King Sinada quickly found another witch doctor to take the place of Mamazda. His name was Akamuza. Mamazda had been tall, dignified and fearless. Akamuza was small and timid. He reminded people of a snake. He must have been sixty years of age at least, but you would guess he was not more that forty. At first, he said only what he knew the king wanted to hear. He agreed with everything Sinanda said and repeated the same words to the king two or three days later.

He told the king, 'You will rule forever. I see it in the sand.'

He saw in the sand everything the king wanted him to see. If the king thought someone was plotting against him, the sand told him that he was right. If the king wanted a new helicopter or a higher wall round the palace, the sand said it was wise.

The king rewarded Akamuza. He gave Akamuza a small house in the palace grounds. He could also call on the king at any time. Akamuza began to whisper more secrets in the king's ear.

One night, near twelve o'clock, Akamuza hurried to the palace and asked to see the king. The servants knew the king's orders.

'Your Majesty,' Akamuza started nervously, 'I've had a dream.'

'Well?' said the king, still half asleep. 'Quickly. Was it about me? Was it about the future?'

'Yes, Your Majesty,' Akamuza said. 'I – I – '

'Oh, for goodness' sake,' shouted the king. 'Out with it!'

Akamuza knew that his acting was very good. King Sinanda could not wait to hear the dream.

'The dream said,' Akamuza paused again, 'the dream said that all kings have enemies. People are always jealous of kings. They are always plotting against kings, even great kings like Your Majesty.'

'Yes, go on,' said Sinanda.

'Every great king–like you, Your Majesty–is meant to rule forever.' Akamuza watched the king's face carefully. 'It is enemies that shorten a king's reign.'

'The dream is right,' said Sinanda. 'I am meant to rule forever. What did your dream say I must do? Well? What did the dream say?'

Akamuza took a deep breath. Then he moved closer to the king's bed and spoke very quietly.

'You must get rid of your enemies,' he said. 'Get rid of them. In the dream I saw–I saw tombstones ... There were no prisoners, only tombstones. And on the tombstones were the names of you enemies.'

'You saw names,' shouted Sinanda. 'You saw names. More enemies! Will they ever end? Will they never let me rule in peace?'

Sinanda sat staring at Akamuza. He burned with anger.

The witch doctor's voice whispered in his head. It seemed to fill his mind with wild ideas.

'Prison is too good for them,' Akamuza whispered. 'They can come back and plot again. Do you want them to return? Do you want them to come back? Kill them, once and for all. Finish the matter now!'

A cunning look came into Sinada's eyes. He smiled an evil smile.

'That's no problem,' he said. 'Just remember their names, the names on the tombstones. Just give me their names and I will deal with them. Every one of them.' His voice rose to a great shout.

He looked about him as if wakening from a deep sleep.

'I must rest now,' Sinanda said. 'I have work to do in the morning.'

Akamuza looked at King Sinanda for a moment and then left the room. Sinanda took a bottle of red and yellow capsules from under his pillow. To help him sleep, the doctor had prescribed two capsules just before the king went to bed. Now he took five or even six to try to sleep. But how could he sleep when he was surrounded by enemies? No matter how many he killed, there always seemed to be more waiting to plot against him. He had not left the palace since the night Mamazda had died. He did not dare leave the palace until all his enemies were dead.

He took eight capsules and finally began to feel drowsy.

'Give me their names!' he said to the silent room.

Two days later, Akamuza came to the king's room. He was carrying a piece of paper with a long list of names on it.

He handed it to the king and bowed.

'These are the names I read on the tombstones,' he said. Akamuza had a strange, staring look in his eye. This list was the death warrant for many people. Akamuza had great power now. The power had affected his mind. Akamuza was no longer completely sane.

Sinanda read the list over once and then read it again. He looked worried.

'But these people are all Gammans,' said Sinanda, recognising many of the names. 'People will say I am a Gamman hater, that I want to kill all the Gammans in Bamanga. That would be genocide.'

Akamuza laughed a low evil laugh.

'Are you afraid of what people will say? These people are your enemies. They want you dead, remember that! They want the king dead!'

Sinanda said, 'Do you mean I shall have to kill a whole people – the Gammans of Bamanga – to rule forever?'

'Or they will kill you. There is no other way.' Akamuza laughed his evil laugh again. 'If you want to rule forever, you must kill, you must torture, you must destroy all those against you ...' Akamuza's laugh made his face ugly. His tongue ran in and out between his lips. If a cobra could laugh, the sound would be like Akamuza's laughter.

The terrible laughter sounded in Sinanda's ears long after Akamuza had left the room. Each time Sinanda gave orders for another victim to be killed, he heard that mocking laugh.

Sinanda followed Akamuza's dream at once. The people whose names were in the list were arrested. Often the king gave no reason for the arrest. Sometimes they were arrested on suspicion of plotting against the king. All were detained in army prisons. There they were tortured and beaten. Then they would be transferred to a tougher prison outside Port Bamanga. The beatings and torture continued. The prisoners would be transferred again, until finally nothing more would be heard of them.

When he had finished with the names on the list, he turned to people he knew well. Many of them were friends. Some of them had fought beside him. He would invite them to the palace for dinner or a glass of beer. None of them ever left the palace. Some were thrown to the crocodiles in the lake in the palace zoo. Others were taken out under cover of darkness and thrown in the sea or buried far from Port Bamanga. He even killed his wife's sister. She had told Mirama that Sinanda was not as well liked among the Bamans as he had been a year earlier.

Next, he turned to the relatives of Fernando the Third. He was afraid on of them might claim the throne again one day. He killed every member of Fernando's family he could find – brothers, sisters, uncles, aunts, nephews, nieces, everyone. Finally, he killed all those who had helped to make him king. Many of them had been with him on the night of the raid and had shown him the way to the throne. He did not want them to try to do what he had done.

When word of the killings got to the neighbouring countries, many people asked why the Bamangans did not rebel and overthrow King Sinanda. The answer was simple. Sinanda had formed a special battalion of soldiers which he called the Special Action Unit. The recruits to the SAU were the best trained and armed group in the country. They were also the fiercest and toughest soldiers. They received higher pay and lived in better conditions than the rest of the army. As a result, they were completely faithful to Sinanda.

They struck terror into all those who saw them. Sinanda had given them black uniforms and black steel helmets. They were highly trained and went around in platoons of fifty men protecting the king and hunting down Sinanda's enemies. Their main tasks were to protect the king at all times and kill important Gammans on Akamuza's list. They also had to make sure to leave no trace of them. But this was not enough. Soon the king ordered them to kill anyone who said anything against him and the way he was ruling the country.

At first, they followed their instructions carefully. But soon the smell of blood entered their heads, and they began to act like madmen. No one was safe from them, and they no longer cared what people said.

11

Sergeant Sinanda stood up in his army Land Rover and looked at the countryside around him. Behind him Corporal Sikiwa stood in another Land Rover looking in the same direction. Captain Haniya was in command of the light tank which had stopped further up the track.

Fernando the Second had captured a long piece of land from Rulindi, the country on Bamanga's north-western border, in a frontier war many years before. Rulindi still claimed the land, and the President of Rulindi had announced that Bamanga must return the land immediately or there would be war. Gold and uranium had been discovered in the west of Bamanga in 1955. King Fernando the Third was sure that the deposits they had found in Bamanga ran into Rulindi through the disputed territory. He had no intention of giving the land back to Rulindi until all the gold and uranium had been extracted.

Captain Haniya's company was on patrol in the

disputed territory. On Sinanda's left was Rulindi. On his right, in the distance, were the great mountains of earth that had been extracted from the gold mines. Bamanga had a larger army than Rulindi, but there was also a dispute on the eastern frontier and soldiers were required to defend Bamanga there. The Bamangan generals did not think that Rulindi would attack, but they had moved some of their best troops up to the border. It was better to be safe than sorry.

Sinanda pointed to a spot ahead of them and to their right.

'There's a dust cloud, sir,' he shouted. 'It's probably the wind, but we should go and look.'

The captain did not like Sinanda giving orders, but in this case he was right. They would have to make sure that the dust cloud was not caused by Rulindi soldiers. He waved the Land Rovers to follow and slid down into the tank. It was very hot in the tank, so he kept the great round cover open to allow the fresh air in. The Land Rovers spread out behind the tank. They drove off the track and started to cross the rocky desert.

'They're army vehicles,' shouted Sinanda. 'They look like jeeps. They're not ours. There are four of them.'

'Spread out further,' ordered Captain Haniya, through the radio. 'I'll go straight for them. Sinanda and Sikiwa, you come in from the sides.'

The tank raced across the desert, its gun pointing at the Rulindi jeeps.

'Fire when you are ready,' Captain Haniya told the tank gunner.

The gunner fired twice, but he missed both times. The machine guns began to fire and one of the soldiers on Sinanda's Land Rover cried out and fell off the moving vehicle. He lay on the ground, his back covered in blood. The tank's big gun fired again and one of the Rulindi jeeps burst into flames and rolled over.

But suddenly there was danger. The two Rulindi jeeps driving towards the tank passed on either side. Captain Haniya tried to close the tank's cover. He was too late. Rulindi soldiers threw three hand grenades into the tank as they drove past. The hand grenades exploded and then all the bombs and ammunition in the tank exploded. The tank became a great ball of fire. Sinanda stared in amazement at the death of the tank and the men in it. He heard shouting in his ear. It was Sikiwa calling to him on the radio.

'You're in charge now ... What do we do?' he shouted.

At first Sinanda could not think. His mind was still full of the flames leaping from the tank. He looked around and tried to make a decision.

'Get us together,' shouted Sikiwa in his headphones. 'Use the Land Rovers as a defence. Quickly! We can still get them.'

Sinanda waved his hand over his head to show that he wanted them to come together. As they slowed down, Sinanda fired his machine gun at one of the Rulindi jeeps. A tyre burst and the jeep nearly turned over before it stopped. Sinanda was frightened, but the idea of shooting at other men filled him with excitement. As soon as they stopped the vehicles their shooting became more accurate. The driver of the third Rulindi jeep was killed, and the vehicle stopped close to Sinanda's defences. Several more Rulindi soldiers were killed before they could escape.

The Rulindi jeep with the burst tyre was very dangerous. Two Rulindi soldiers tried to fix the wheel. Their comrades shot at Sinanda's defences to keep them quiet.

The Rulindi soldiers in the third jeep tried to pull the dead driver from behind the steering wheel. But every time they tried, Sinanda's men shot at them, hitting two of them.

Sikiwa pointed at the last Rulindi jeep. It had stopped outside the range of Sinanda's bullets and was preparing to fire small bombs at them. He shouted that he would stop them.

Taking one gunner, he drove one of the Land Rovers as fast as he could towards the enemy vehicle. The gunner shot as they drove. One of the Rulindi soldiers shot at the vehicle as it came up to him. The windscreen was shattered and Sikiwa fell over the steering wheel, dead. Sikiwa's Land Rover crashed into the Rulindi vehicle, and both exploded in a mass of flames.

Sinanda watched in horror. He didn't care for Sikiwa as a friend, but Sikiwa was the only person who talked to him and treated him like a human being. They had killed something that belonged to him, Sinanda. With a shout of rage, he took one of the heavy machine guns and ran across the desert firing at the broken-down jeep. He killed the five soldiers behind the jeep and then turned to the two men trying to repair the wheel. They started to put their hands up. Sinanda shot them over and over again. He felt wonderful. He smiled as he turned back to his men. He had never felt so good.

The two remaining Rulindi soldiers put their hands up and walked towards Sinanda and his men.

Taking his revolver, Sinanda shot each of them in the chest and the head.

'That's for our friends and countrymen,' he shouted loudly. 'That's for Sikiwa and the others.'

The stories of Sinanda's bravery soon reached the ears of very senior officers and even the king himself. No one mentioned how he had killed the last two Rulindi soldiers. The soldiers had started to exaggerate what had happened. Sinanda had killed forty and then fifty men and had rescued his company from certain death. Although the stories were exaggerated, there seemed to be no doubt that Sinanda was a hero again. Also, the fight in the desert had shocked the President of Rulindi. He called for a cease-fire and agreed to sign a peace treaty with Fernando the Third.

The deaths of Captain Haniya and three lieutenants in an ambush earlier in the border war meant that the army was short of junior officers. At the end of Sinanda's seventh year in the army, the colonel called Sinanda to his office. When Sinanda left the office, he had become a lieutenant. He was the third Timangan to be an officer in the Royal Bamangan Army.

12

When he had started the killing, King Sinanda had wanted to strike terror into the hearts of his subjects. He was determined that no one would oppose him. He would rule Bamanga forever. If he had to kill, then he would.

And the killing continued.

Once the killing began, it could not be stopped. Killing gave birth to more killing. The Special Action Unit, in their dark uniforms, black boots and steel helmets, and carrying automatic weapons, terrorised all the people of Bamanga. No one was safe from them.

The people, especially the Gammans, were afraid to protest about the brutal behaviour of the SAU. When they protested at first, they were arrested and questioned. Many of those arrested simply disappeared. People stopped complaining. They did not even talk to their friends. Even their friends could be spying for Sinanda. Bamanga was full of the king's spies. There were spies in the offices, in the markets among the market women, among families, everywhere. Everyone suspected everyone else. Friends no longer trusted each other. Too many people had disappeared as a result of a careless conversation.

Although there was no curfew and the sun did not go down until seven o'clock, all the streets were deserted by six o'clock. People were not safe in their houses, but they were less safe in the streets after dark. If the SAU saw anyone out after dark, they were free to arrest that person and question him. And still people disappeared.

At first the SAU disposed of the bodies secretly. They took them far out to sea or buried them in the marshes in the south-east or in the desert in the north of the country. But soon they became bolder. They no longer bothered to dispose of some of the bodies. Soon Port Bamanga became a city of fear and death. Some mornings, two or three dead bodies could be seen lying in the streets. Some mornings it was more. People would recognise the bodies of their friends, but they could do nothing. Children on their way to school held their noses at the terrible smell.

Vultures hovered over the city all the time now. They roosted on rooftops, on baobab trees or just walked along the roads. They seemed to know that no one would come to collect the bodies. They became so bold that passers-by would turn their heads to avoid looking at vultures pecking at the dead bodies.

No one in Bamanga dared to challenge Sinanda and his SAU. He was supreme. There was nobody to question his actions any more. Although he still did not leave the palace grounds, he knew that he was king forever. It became a song which echoed in his head. He sang it in his bath in the morning. He sang it to himself in the mirror as he brushed his teeth and combed his hair. A great king should look beautiful, he thought. A king forever had to look beautiful.

Sinanda knew he had killed all his enemies in Bamanga. He forgot he might have enemies outside Bamanga. When the killings grew worse and worse, many people fled from Bamanga. Many fled to Rulindi and other neighbouring countries. They told stories of the terrible events in Bamanga. Although this had happened before in Africa, most people believed that the stories were exaggerated. No one would behave in this way today, they said. However, newspapers all over the world heard about the stories and some decided to send journalists to investigate them.

The king's Personal Assistant received a letter signed with the name Marie Jordaine. She explained that she was a journalist with a French newspaper. She wanted to have an interview with the king to discuss the development of the country since the death of Fernando the Third.

The king's Personal Assistant knew that Sinanda hated journalists, so he invited Miss Jordaine to call on him to discuss her request. Miss Jordaine was a beautiful young woman who smiled at the Personal Assistant and repeated her request. The PA asked for a list of the questions she wanted to ask the king. Miss Jordaine took a list from her bag. The PA explained that if the king agreed to see her, she must not change any of the questions. She said she understood. The PA told her he would ring her at her hotel to tell her when the king would see her.

When Sinanda saw the list of his appointments for the next day, he saw the word journalist immediately. He looked at the PA angrily. But when the PA explained that she was young, beautiful and French, Sinanda smiled and ticked her name.

Marie Jordaine arrived early for her appointment. She sat outside the PA's office for two hours. Just when she thought the king was not going to see her, the PA appeared and took her along a corridor and into the king's sitting room.

Sinanda appeared immediately and invited her to take tea with him. He then asked her about her visit. She explained again that she worked for a Paris newspaper. Her editor was eager to find out how Bamanga had developed since the death of Fernando the Third. Many people had heard about Bamanga's gold and uranium, and about the recent discovery of diamonds in the north. France bought Bamangan beef and hides and the French government was ready to improve trade links with the king.

Sinanda answered the questions she asked, just as they had appeared on her list. Then he asked if there was anything else he could do. She asked him if it would be possible to spend three days travelling around the country looking at the industries. Sinanda promised to have a car at the hotel next morning to take her round. They shook hands and she left.

Sinanda called General Bogada, the commander of the Special Action Unit. He asked the general to make sure that Miss Jordaine was taken to see the various industries in the country.

'Make sure she only sees factories and shops,' he ordered. 'I don't want pictures all over the newspapers.'

'Don't worry,' said General Bogada. 'I'll send two of my best men with her.'

'Just take her around and then put her on an aeroplane,' Sinanda said.

Marie Jordaine took notes of all her visits. She also took pictures and asked the people she saw questions. No one answered her. They saw the SAU men and refused to speak to her. Marie had two cameras. She had a large one which she used in front of the SAU officers. But she had another tiny camera which she hid in her clothing. She used this camera to take pictures of all the most terrible sights in Port Bamanga and in the countryside.

Three days later the SAU officers took her to the airport and put her on a plane for Europe. Before they left her, they took her notes, her camera and the pictures she had taken with it. They did not find her little camera or the tiny rolls of film she had taken.

Marie Jordaine wrote a long report for her

newspaper. She described the terrible conditions in Bamanga. Along with her report were many pictures showing what was happening in Bamanga. They had all been taken by the tiny camera she had hidden in her clothes.

Other newspapers from all over the world printed the story and showed the pictures. The report appeared in America, in Britain and in Europe. People read it and wondered if these terrible things could happen in this day and age. Governments all over the world began to ask questions. People who had fled from Bamanga asked the International Red Cross to help. The Red Cross decided to fly food and medicine into Bamanga as soon as possible.

The question of Bamanga was raised in the United Nations, and the Secretary-General consulted with member nations about a meeting to discuss Bamanga. But it was in the meeting of the Organisation of African Unity in Addis Ababa that the question of Bamanga was first raised.

It so happened that the Chairman for that year was Bamanga. King Sinanda did not go to Ethiopia, but sent General Bogada, the commander of the Special Action Unit, and some advisers instead.

'Let me tell everyone before this meeting starts,' said General Bogada, 'that we will not discuss the affairs of Bamanga. What happens in our country is none of your business. We will not discuss it.'

'Please,' said the President of Tanzania, 'please understand that we are only trying to help. Our brothers from Bamanga are wrong to stop us. People in your country are dying. There is a terrible dictator in Bamanga. The Bamangan people are our brothers. In Africa everyone must help his neighbour. We must discuss the killings of our brothers and sisters in Bamanga and try to find an answer to their suffering.'

General Bogada banged the table in a rage.

'I have told you there will be no interference,' he shouted. 'Keep out of our affairs! I must insist! Keep out! Bamanga is Chairman of the OAU this year. I say the matter is closed.'

The hall fell silent. General Bogada rose to his feet and began to walk out of the conference hall. At the door he turned and looked at each of the members in turn.

'How many of you are angels?' he cried in a high voice.

Under his breath he muttered, 'Hypocrites!' but many of the people near him heard what he said. He looked around the room again and banged the door closed behind him.

Everyone tried to speak at once in the conference hall. There was so much noise no one could be heard. The meeting broke up in confusion.

A week later the International Red Cross flew into King Sinanda Airport outside Port Bamanga. Three boeing 747s carried food, medicine and clothing. Three members of the SAU met them at the aeroplane steps. They were wearing their steel helmets and carried AK47 rifles.

'Stay where you are,' called the officer in charge. 'You are not to leave the plane.'

The Red Cross Director of Operations was a small English woman with blonde hair and a serious face.

'We have brought food and medicine and clothing for the suffering people of Bamanga,' she called back. 'You cannot stop us giving these things to your people.'

The officer waved his rifle at her angrily.

'Madam, I warn you ...' He pointed the rifle straight at her. 'Leave Bamangans to settle their own problems. There is no emergency in Bamanga, no war ... So get out! And don't come back!'

'What about the wounded and the dying? What happens to them? Will you just let them die in the streets?' The Red Cross Director spoke in a gentle voice.

'Wounded? What wounded? Dying? What dying?' The officer held out his arms and looked all around him.

The officer stared at her for a moment and then turned and walked away. He strode quickly through the airport lounge with his men on either side. People moved out of their way. The officer climbed into his Land Rover and drove off.

The Red Cross Director stood in the doorway of the 747. She looked out at the airport buildings. The Chief Immigration Officer came to the bottom of the steps.

'Have you a visa to enter Bamanga?' he asked her.

'No,' she said. 'We are just bringing food and medicine to help your people.'

'If you have no visa, you cannot enter Bamanga.'

It was true. The Red Cross could not enter Bamanga. The United Nations and the OAU were helpless too. If they were not invited to enter Bamanga, there was nothing they could do. The people of Bamanga must help themselves, if they could.

13

Colonel Sinanda sat in his office planning the exercises for his men for the next week. Outside Sergeant Garanga was training his men in the fields. Sinana smiled to himself. He remembered the first time he met Garanga. He had been to see Mirama and talk about their wedding plans. On the way back to the army camp he saw four or five men arguing with a tall soldier. Suddenly they all jumped forward and began to hit him. Sinanda stopped. He did not care about the soldier, but he always got pleasure out of beating people. He picked up a heavy bar and ran over to the fight. He hit one of the men on the back of the head with the bar. The man fell to the ground without a sound. Sinanda hit another man on the back and then smashed the bar into his face. The man screamed with pain. The soldier had knocked one of the men down. The others ran away when they saw Sinanda's metal bar.

The soldier looked at his rescuer, and then tidied

himself quickly when he saw it was an officer. He stood at attention and saluted.

'Corporal Garanga, sir, from the First Regiment,' he said. 'Thank you, sir, for saving me. I think they were going to kill me.'

'I'm Captain Sinanda,' Sinanda told him. 'Report to me at headquarters in the morning.' Then he turned and walked on towards the camp. Garanga came slowly after him.

Next morning Garanga reported to Captain Sinanda's office.

'You look as if you enjoy a fight,' Sinada told him. 'I'm going to get you transferred to my company, if you would like that.'

'Oh yes, sir,' said Garanga. 'Then I can thank you for saving my life. Maybe one day I can save your life.'

Colonel Sinanda smiled again. That had been five years ago. Garanga was still the only person he trusted in the whole of Bamanga.

Sinanda had another reason to smile at Garanga. It was Garanga who had given him the idea. Garanga had reported to his office the previous day. He had complained about the behaviour of the men. The other officers did not train the men properly. Even the king did not seem to worry when he came to inspect the soldiers.

'You would do better,' Garanga said. 'You would

make sure the army behaved like an army and not like a lot of old women. If only we could make you king!'

Sinanda looked at Garanga with a strange look in his eyes.

'What did you say?' Sinanda asked. 'Say that again.'

'I didn't mean any harm,' Garanga spoke quickly. 'I only said you would make a far better king. But it's true, you would.'

Sinanda waved for Garanga to leave the room. Then he stood looking out of the window. He thought about Garanga's idea. He liked it. The more he thought about it, the more he liked it. But could he do it? Could he become king? No, it wasn't possible. He would need help. The other officers did not like him enough. Then he started to think of the plan. It was a plan which he had thought about for a long time. Garanga's words now made him think about it again.

Sinanda picked three officers he knew well. He also knew they were not honest. For weeks, he talked to them about the army. He talked about the generals. How much money they made. How they only promoted their friends to the best positions. Then he talked to Garanga. He told Garanga what he was going to do.

'I told you, didn't I?' Garanga said. 'What do you want me to do?'

'I want you to find as many men as you can who will help us,' said Sinanda. 'We need men who will fight the king and his guards. Tell them we need to change things. The people are tired of Fernando and his relatives and his big houses. All that money he sends to banks overseas. Bamangans can use that money to make the country better.'

The three officers seen found other colonels and junior officers who would help them. Sinanda promised each of them promotion and good jobs when he became king.

Soon they had enough men to start to plan for the attack on the palace. Sinanda and the other colonels began to transfer their men to the regiments which they commanded. Then they arranged for the regiments to be moved to army barracks in or near Port Bamanga. They explained that they wanted to practise special methods of attack. They needed to use these regiments because they had the tanks and the other equipment for these special tactics. The generals had received a lot of new equipment from France and Britain. They were delighted that the junior officers were eager to learn to use it.

The last step was to make sure that the Gamman soldiers, who might be loyal to King Fernando, were in the north-west of the country at the time of Sinanda's attack of Fernando's palace. The last of Sinanda's soldiers came down from the north. They reported that they had seen a Rulindi regiment near the border. Fernando immediately sent a Gamman regiment to patrol the area.

Fernando was having a great dinner to celebrate twenty-five years on the throne of Bamanga. All the important people in the country were invited. These included generals, politicians, ambassadors and other foreign guests. After the dinner there were singers and jugglers and traditional dancers to entertain the guests. Then the guests were allowed to dance and drink and talk. None of the plotters had been invited to the dinner. They were making their final preparations to attack the palace. They would move as soon as the last guest had left and the last person in the palace had gone to bed. Sinanda was sure that everyone would be too tired to guard the palace properly.

At a quarter past three one of the soldiers reported that the last light in the palace had just been turned out. Sinanda gave instructions for the attack to start at four o'clock exactly. Sinanda's regiment would move into position at half past three. The second regiment would attack the back of the palace, and the tank regiment would wait in the barracks close to the palace until the attack had started. Sinanda did not want the noise of the tanks to warn the soldiers in the palace. The second tank regiment, waiting outside the city, would capture all the communications buildings in the city.

At five minutes to four, Sinanda and Garanga were waiting across the road from the main entrance to the palace. At four o'clock one of their big guns would blow down the gates and the soldiers would attack. At the rear of the palace the second regiment waited to climb the walls and attack the army barracks inside the palace grounds.

Just before four o'clock the air was filled with the noise of the tanks starting their engines. This wakened one of the guards. He looked out and saw soldiers crawling along the wall opposite the palace. He sounded the alarm. At that moment Sinanda signalled for his men to start the attack.

Many of the soldiers inside the palace grounds were either asleep or sleepy. Some of them were drunk. The noise of the big gun blowing up the main gates and the sound of the tanks in the streets outside quickly wakened them. They rushed to defend the palace, pulling on trousers, putting on helmets and loading guns as they ran.

Sinanda's men rushed to make the first attack. They entered the grounds of the palace and started to advance on the buildings. There was one piece of bad luck. The alarm had been given in time for the tank traps to be opened. Great holes appeared in the roads around the palace and at the gates. The tanks could not move. But the men of the second regiment had captured two of the buildings at the rear of the palace and were preparing to move forward.

Messengers arrived to tell Sinanda that the radio and television stations, the post office and the airport had been captured without a fight. All the army barracks around Port Bamanga were already under Sinanda's command. Tanks had surrounded the parliament buildings. The port had also been closed.

Eight hours later Garanga and a special unit

captured the guardhouse which controlled the tank traps. As soon as they were closed, the tanks moved forward. Their guns blew great holes in the walls of the army barracks and the soldiers inside soon surrendered. In another four hours Sinanda's regiment was attacking the great doors at the front of the palace. A bomb finally blew one of the doors off its hinges and the soldiers advanced behind the cover of the tanks. There was a final charge up the hundred steps to the palace doors. At the same time the second regiment broke into the palace at the back. Sinanda and Garanga raced up the steps with the other members of the regiment. Half-way up, Garanga gave a shout and fell holding on to his leg. Sinanda looked back at Garanga lying on the ground. He ordered two men to look after him and ran on up the steps. As he reached the top the last of the soldiers inside the palace put down their weapons and surrendered. There was silence for a moment and then Sinanda's men started to cheer.

They put Sinanda up on their shoulders and carried him into the palace. They took him to the great hall of the palace. At one end was a huge chair made of iroko wood. They took him to the chair and made him sit in it. About his shoulders they put the black leopardskins of Bamanga and on his head they put the gold and ivory crown.

'Long live the king! Long live the king!' they shouted.

It took them two hours to find King Fernando. Some soldiers had gone down to the cellars to look for drink. There under one of the tables in the cold darkness they found Fernando. They took him to Sinanda who was working hard to make sure that the city and the rest of the country was under his command.

'What's the meaning of this? What do you think you are doing?' Fernando tried to hide his fear.

Sinanda did not look at him. He turned to one of the colonels.

'You know what to do?' Sinanda asked him. The colonel nodded and then he signalled to his men to bring Fernando. Sinanda smiled as they dragged the king out of the room.

14

'All my enemies are dead,' said King Sinanda. He smiled at Queen Mirama. 'I'm free! I can go where I want. I can do what I want. I can go wherever I want in Bamanga. Why should I remain locked up in the palace?'

Mirama watched him as he walked about the room. Her worry showed on her face.

'Remember what Mamazda said,' she reminded the king. 'He said, if you want to rule forever –'

'Mamazda is dead.'

'But the truth is alive! Everyone knows ...'

'I have my Special Action Unit. I have security,' said Sinanda.

'There is no security against death.' Mirama started to sob. 'Don't go out! Please!'

Sinanda did not seem to hear her last words. He stared at her angrily.

'So you want me to die?' His eyes started to gleam with anger.

'I want you to live long. That is why I want you to stay inside the palace grounds. Please, stay at home!'

'On whose side are you O Queen? Their side, or my side?'

'I want you to live. Don't challenge the gods. Remember what Mamazda said. Remember the message in the sand.' She was starting to cry now. 'What do you want to go into Port Bamanga for? Don't you have all you wish for here in the palace?'

'How can I rule the people if I do not see them? How can I make things better if I do not know what is wrong?'

'But you are ruling them,' she cried. 'Things are beginning to get better, aren't they?'

Sinanda paid to attention to what Queen Mirama was saying. He was determined to see his country. He was determined to drive into Port Bamanga, to let his people see him. He called General Bogada to a meeting.

'I want to tighten the security. I have to start going around the country. I want the people to see me. I want to see my country. We must double the number of men in the SAU. If you have more men, you can protect me better.'

General Bogada watched King Sinanda as he walked about the room. The king never seemed to sit down. He was always moving about. General Bogada believed the king was going mad. Maybe it was time for a new king.

'I'll need more money,' General Boganda said.

'More men means more money. Better protection means more money.'

'Yes, yes,' said the king. 'I'll get you more money. Just make sure you get more men.'

Sinanda ordered the Minister of Trade to sell more of the diamonds from the mines in the north. This would allow the Minister of Finance to pay General Bogada for the extra soldiers.

The Minister of Finance came to the palace to remind the king that Bamanga still owed the World Bank the interest on their loan of four hundred and fifty million dollars. The king removed him from his office and appointed another politician in his place.

'I know I have to pay the World Bank. I know that. But pay for my security first,' he ordered the new minister.

General Bogada immediately received the money he needed.

Queen Mirama was not happy when she heard the news.

'I think you are wrong,' she said. 'I think you have made a mistake.'

'You mean because I am safer?'

'No. But General Bogada is stronger now. He has more soldiers than all your other generals. I do not trust him. I think he wants to be king.'

'Bogada is my friend. I trust him.'

'I don't understand,' she said. 'Until now you trusted nobody in Bamanga. Now you trust this man. Why? He's not Timangan. Why do you trust him?'

Sinanda ignored her fears.

'With more soldiers, I am safer. Bogada is only a general. The men obey the king. They know they are here to protect me. If anyone is plotting against me, it must be someone else.'

Two days later, the king and his son were walking in the palace grounds. Three Special Action Unit soldiers were protecting them. Suddenly there was a shot. Danta gave a scream and fell to the ground. There was a second shot. One of the soldiers had stepped in front of the king. The bullet hit him in the face. He was dead before his body hit the ground. The soldiers fired at the place where the shots came from, but the killer escaped.

Danta was rushed to the palace hospital. The doctor told the king that it was just a flesh wound. He bandaged it carefully and Danta was carried home to his mother. Garanga appeared at that moment, a worried look on his face.

'I'm sorry,' he said, 'I was sleeping. I was wakened by the shots.'

Sinanda's SAU searched the palace grounds again. They found nothing. Sinanda then went to see the soldier's body. It was lying in one of the rooms in the palace barracks. The king stood quietly for a long time.

'I'll kill the man who killed you, my friend.'

Sinanda went back to the palace. Mirama was waiting for him.

'Did you find the man who did it?' she asked him.

Sinanda shook his head. Then he went into a rage.

He walked up and down, smashing anything he could find.

'I'll find him! I'll find him! He killed one of my guards. If people think they can kill my SAU–' he shouted.

'Yes,' said the queen. 'But more important, he almost killed you. How could he get into the palace without being seen? Where was the SAU? Where were the security men?'

Sinanda looked at the queen. His eyes filled with suspicion.

'You mean, you mean ... ?' The king looked at Queen Mirama. 'Who else can it be? Who else? I know he wants to be king. I've been suspicious of him for weeks.'

The queen said nothing for a long time.

'What will you do?' she asked at last.

'Don't worry,' Sinanda said. 'He won't harm us ever again.'

Twenty-four hours later, the body of Sergeant Garanga was found floating in Port Bamanga harbour. He had been shot nine times.

15

Queen Mirama decided to make one last attempt to get her husband to stop all the terrible things which had been happening in Bamanga. She went to him early one evening.

'My husband,' she said, 'ever since Mamazda died, you have been very unhappy. There has been no peace.'

She stopped and looked at him.

'All this blood!' she cried. 'I hate blood.'

'You mean the death of Garanga? He was trying to kill me and your son. What was Garanga to you? Was he your brother? Was he your friend?'

'Garanga was a poor soldier who helped you to become king,' Queen Mirama said. 'You became king, and you have rewarded him and all the others with death. How do you know that it was Garanga who tried to kill you?' It could have been General Bogada, but you think he can do no wrong.'

She was crying now, tears running down her face.

'All the people who fought on your side. Where are they?' She stared at him. 'All dead! All dead!'

The king hated to be reminded of all the killings. They were something he had to do. He did not like the queen's behaviour. She should not talk so much. What he had done was for her good too.

He turned and walked to the window. If she continued to talk like this she would have to be killed too. He realised this now. His eyes started to glare with rage.

Queen Mirama went to her bedroom. She fell on her knees and put her head in her hands.

'Dear God,' she prayed aloud, 'grant this man, my husband, eyes to see and ears to hear. Let him see the evil he is doing. Please, make him see sense before he goes mad with all the blood he has spilt. Let him see he is doing wrong. Let him hear the cries of his people. Please, please, God.'

Sinanda stood behind her, his glaring eyes watching her. As she raised her head, he rushed forward and seized her by the throat. He squeezed and squeezed. She could not cry out. She struggled and struggled. Then her body gave a horrible shake. It relaxed and she slipped to the floor.

Sinanda's face was running with sweat.

He went to the bathroom and washed his face and hands carefully. He stood for a long time looking in the mirror. Then he pressed a bell. The new Chief of Security came into the room.

'Queen Mirama has just died,' Sinanda said quietly.

'The queen has just died,' the Chief of Security repeated.

Sinanda turned to his wife and took her pretty head in his hands. He turned her over gently. The lifeless eyes looked at him. He laid the head down and closed the eyes which seemed to stare at him accusingly.

Servants came and placed the body on the bed. They would prepare her for burial later. The king sat at her dressing table. He combed his hair. He loved to comb his hair, to look good all the time.

Three days later he called General Bogada to him.

'I'm going to inspect Port Bamanga tonight,' he said. 'I want the car ready for seven o'clock.'

'Yes, Your Majesty,' General Bogada saluted. 'I'll have the SAU ready.'

That evening as darkness fell, Sinanda dressed himself in his finest uniform. It was the uniform of a field marshal. The king had promoted himself the month before. His chest was covered in medals.

He walked to the doors of the palace and looked at the SAU men lined up outside. The guard commander saluted.

'No sirens,' he said. 'No outriders. Just one Land Rover in front and one behind.'

Sinanda got into the car and the driver drove out of the palace grounds. They drove through the gates and into the city.

As they drove, he listened to the sounds of Port Bamanga. He smiled happily. Maybe after his drive into the city his mind would be at rest. Maybe he would find peace.

The little procession moved through the city. There were no crowds, no shouting. They came to the main square, with the great cathedral on one side and the banks and offices on the others. The car stopped.

'Why have we stopped?' Sinanda called to the SAU officer sitting beside the driver. The officer said nothing.

'What do you think you are doing? Drive on,' Sinanda shouted angrily. Still the officer did not turn.

Sinanda opened the door and got out of the car. He looked around. There was nobody in the square. He looked for a long time at the city he had not seen for four years.

There was a shot. Sinanda looked down at the dark stain on his chest in surprise. Then he felt the pain and he fell to the ground. The SAU guards ran up and quickly pushed his body back into the car.

General Bogada marched out of the darkness. He looked at Sinada's body lying on the floor of the car. He took his pistol from its holster, held it to the king's head, and pulled the trigger. He nodded to the SAU men. They got into the car and drove off into the night.

Next morning General Bogada went on Bamanga radio to announce that Sinanda had been overthrown and that he had become king. He would take the title Fernando the Fourth.

The king who had wanted to rule forever was never heard of again. King Sinanda had forgotten one thing. It is only death that rules forever.

Questions

1. Where did Sinanda come from? What did his father do?
2. How did he come to join the army?
3. Why was he promoted to sergeant?
4. How did he get promoted to lieutenant?
5. What three things did Sinanda build or add to the palace when he became king?
6. Why did he make Garanga Head of Security?
7. Who did he make Commander of the Special Action Unit? What this a good choice?
8. Why did his mother and father say they wanted to go back to Timanga? What was the real reason?
9. Why did Sinanda kill Mamazda?
10. Why did Sinanda start to kill all the Gammans in Bamanga?
11. Why did Mamazda tell Sinanda he should never leave the palace?
12. Why could Sinanda not be king forever?

ACTIVITIES

1. Which part of the book did you find most exciting? Write a short account of the most exciting part in your own words. Then explain in two or three sentences why you found it exciting.
2. Write a short description of Garanga. Explain why you did or did not like him.
3. Hold a class discussion. The title of the discussion is: 'How can we do away with dictators?'
4. Draw a picture of King Sinanda in his field marshal's uniform with all the medals on it.

Glossary

administration - a group of people who manage a business or the army
akara - fried bean cake
ambassadors - men sent to represent their country in a foreign country
ambitious - determined to do well
anxious - worried or nervous
appearance - the way a person looks
assemble - put together

barracks - buildings where soldiers live
battalion - group of soldiers, part of a regiment about 1,000 men. A major is in charge of a battalion

company - part of a battalion of soldiers, about 150 men. A captain is in charge of a company
cowered - crouched down in fear

destroy - break or damage something completely
dignity, dignified - behaving in a serious and regal manner
disputed - argued about who owns something

exaggerate - say something is bigger or better than it really is

fascinated - very interested in
flattered - praised someone too much

genocide - killing all the people in the same group or race

improve - make something better

luxury, luxurious - something very expensive not needed for ordinary living

magnificent - very large and beautiful
monarch - another name for a king

oppression - ruling people cruelly and unfairly

plantations - very large farms growing cotton or tobacco and using slaves as workers
platoon - part of a company of soldiers, about 30 men. A lieutenant is in charge of a platoon
plotted - planned secretly together

reception - large party organised to welcome people
recruits - new soldiers, not yet trained
regiment - very large group of soldiers, about 5,000, divided into three or four battalions. A colonel is in charge of a regiment

security - group of people whose job it is to keep buildings or important people safe
shortages - not having enough food, clothes and other things in the shops
splendour - brightness and beauty of a place
superstitious - afraid of the unknown, believing in ghosts and bad luck
suspicious - suspecting a person of doing wrong

tyrant - cruel ruler

About the Author

Cyprian Ekwensi was born in Nigeria in 1921, the son of a famed storyteller and elephant hunter. In early life, he worked as a forestry officer in Nigeria and as a pharmacist in Romford, Essex. On returning home, he wrote his first novel, *People of the City* (1954), which was one of the first Nigerian novels to be published internationally. *Jagua Nana*, his most famous book, appeared in 1961 and won the Dag Hammarskjöld prize in literature, though it was banned in schools and attacked by the church. Later in life, Ekwensi worked in broadcasting, politics, and as a pharmacist, while writing over forty books and scripts. He died in 2007. His works continue to appeal to readers all over the world.

Other Books by Cyprian Ekwensi

People of the City
The Passport of Mallam Ilia
The Drummer Boy
Jagua Nana
Burning Grass
An African Night's Entertainment
Beautiful Feathers
Survive the Peace
Masquerade Time
Restless City and Christmas Gold
Glittering City

Ingram Content Group UK Ltd.
Milton Keynes UK
UKHW010646260723
425809UK00004B/205